DERAIL

Frank, Joe, and Phil raced through the crowds. They made it to the contest hall in less than five minutes. But when they walked inside, something was definitely not right.

"Hey, guys," Joe said. "What's up?"

Everyone turned to stare at Phil. As they backed away from the table, the boys gasped. A huge chunk of the Zooming Zombie Coaster was missing!

THE HARDY BOYS®

SECRET FILES #9

The Great Coaster Caper

ZOOMING! ZOMBIE COASTER

BY **FRANKLIN W. DIXON**

ILLUSTRATED BY **SCOTT BURROUGHS**

ALADDIN • NEW YORK LONDON TORONTO SYDNEY NEW DELHI

This book is a work of fiction. Any references to historical events, real people, or real locales are used fictitiously. Other names, characters, places, and incidents are the product of the author's imagination, and any resemblance to actual events or locales or persons, living or dead, is entirely coincidental.

ALADDIN

An imprint of Simon & Schuster Children's Publishing Division
1230 Avenue of the Americas, New York, NY 10020
First Aladdin paperback edition August 2012
Text copyright © 2012 by Simon & Schuster, Inc.
Illustrations copyright © 2012 by Scott Burroughs
All rights reserved, including the right of reproduction in whole or in part in any form.
ALADDIN is a trademark of Simon & Schuster, Inc., and related logo is a registered trademark of Simon & Schuster, Inc.
THE HARDY BOYS is a registered trademark of Simon & Schuster, Inc.
For information about special discounts for bulk purchases, please contact Simon & Schuster Special Sales at 1-866-506-1949 or business@simonandschuster.com.
The Simon & Schuster Speakers Bureau can bring authors to your live event. For more information or to book an event contact the Simon & Schuster Speakers Bureau at 1-866-248-3049 or visit our website at www.simonspeakers.com.
Designed by Lisa Vega
The text of this book was set in Garamond.
Manufactured in the United States of America 0614 OFF
10 9 8 7 6 5 4 3 2
Library of Congress Control Number 2012938759
ISBN 978-1-4424-1669-7
ISBN 978-1-4424-1670-3 (eBook)

⚞ CONTENTS ⚟

The Great Coaster Caper

1

Buccaneer Bullies

Eight-year-old Joe Hardy gulped as the cage door snapped shut. It wasn't the cage of a snarling tiger or a wild gorilla. It was worse—much worse! Joe was locked inside the Tarantula, the scariest, most extreme ride at the thrill park!

"What am I doing here?" Joe shouted. He had always avoided the Tarantula like cooties.

Joe's nine-year-old brother, Frank, sat across from him inside the cage. "You're not wimping out, are you, Joe?" Frank asked with a smirk.

Joe gripped the safety bar so tightly he thought his knuckles would crack! "No way!" he squeaked. "Bring it!"

Joe's stomach dropped as the cage lifted off the ground. He squeezed his eyes shut. This was it . . .

until he felt the steely black cage jerk to a stop.

Did the ride break down? Joe wondered hopefully.

No such luck. In a flash the cage began spinning until everything around Joe was one big dizzying blur!

"Whoooaaaaaa!" Joe cried through rattling teeth.

"Hold on, bro!" Frank laughed. "We're going to flip!"

Flip? "Why did I let you talk me into this ride, Frank Hardy?" Joe yelled. "I must have been craaaaaaazy—"

"Joe? Joe?" Frank's voice cut in. "Joe, wake up!"

Joe's eyes snapped open. He turned his head to see Frank hanging upside down—from his top bunk, not inside a cage!

With a sigh Joe let his head fall back on his pillow. The terrifying Tarantula ride was only a dream. Or nightmare!

"That must have been some dream," Frank said, flipping down to the floor. "What was it about?"

Joe kept his mouth shut. He had been scared of the Tarantula ride at the Thrill Kingdom amusement park since he was a really little kid. Frank would just tease him like he did all the time.

"Um . . . I had this dream about zombies, Frank!" Joe said, climbing out of bed. "Seven-foot zombies chasing me all through Bayport."

"Zombies, huh?" Frank said. "You don't think it had something do with Phil's Zooming Zombie Coaster? And the contest today?"

Joe smiled at the thought of the contest at Thrill Kingdom. It was a cool contest just for kids. The rules were to design and build a miniature thrill ride. Not only would the winner get free ride passes for the rest of the summer—his or her ride would replace the old fun house, Buccaneer Cove!

"Phil has got to win first prize," Frank said. He pulled a neatly folded polo shirt from his dresser drawer. "It's totally sweet!"

"Because we helped," Joe said. He grabbed a wrinkled T-shirt draped over a chair. "You helped Phil glue Popsicle sticks to make the tracks. And I ate the Popsicles."

To prove it, Joe stuck out his tongue. Even though he had brushed his teeth after eating the last pop the night before, his tongue was still streaked with the colors of Freezy Fruity. Joe was totally sick of Freezy Fruity pops, but not of his cool tie-dyed tongue.

Frank and Joe got dressed, stepping over sports gear, comic books, video games, and sneakers.

Not only did Frank and Joe share a room, they also shared the tree house their father had built for them in the woods behind their house. Besides being a great place to chill, it was also the brothers' secret detective headquarters. When Frank and Joe weren't playing softball, hanging out at the arcade, or doing their homework, they were solving mysteries all over the town of Bayport!

Though Frank and Joe were awesome detectives, sometimes they needed their dad's help. Fenton Hardy was a private investigator, so he knew a thing or two about cracking cases.

"Frank, Joe!" Mrs. Hardy called up the staircase. "Phil and his dad will be here soon. What do you guys want for breakfast? Eggs? Waffles?"

"Anything but Freezy Fruity pops," Joe joked.

It wasn't long before Frank and Joe were sitting in the backseat of the Cohen family car, headed for Thrill Kingdom. Phil sat in the middle, his Zooming Zombie Coaster model on his lap. Each boy wore a badge around his neck that would admit him into Thrill Kingdom for the contest.

"I brought some marbles to roll down the

tracks," Phil said. "To demonstrate the direction the cars would go in."

"Wow!" Frank said, impressed. "Now I know you're going to win, Phil."

"If you win," Joe said slowly, "I mean *when* you win . . ."

"The answer is yes!" Phil sighed. "You guys will get my extra ride passes—I've told you a million times!"

Joe grinned from ear to ear. "Well, if that's the case," he said, "I'm going to ride every ride in the park!"

"As in . . . the Tarantula?" Frank asked.

Joe felt his blood freeze.

"Here's a challenge," Frank told Joe. "If Phil's Zooming Zombie Coaster wins, you'll brave the Tarantula—once and for all!"

"You're still too scared to ride the Tarantula?" Phil asked Joe. "No way!"

"I love that Tarantula!" Mr. Cohen said as he drove the car. "If it weren't for my migraine head-aches, I'd ride it every week!"

"Everybody rides the Tarantula, Joe," Frank declared. "Aunt Gertrude even rode the Tarantula last summer!"

Joe felt his cheeks burn. Their aunt had not only rode the Tarantula, she'd raised both arms above her head and yelled, "Woo-hoooo!"

"Okay, okay!" Joe blurted out. "Deal!"

The brothers reached over Phil's Zooming Zombie Coaster to fist bump.

"What have you got to lose, Joe?" Phil chuckled. "Besides your lunch!"

"Ha-ha," Joe muttered. Maybe Phil wouldn't win. But he *wanted* Phil to win. And he *definitely* wanted those free passes to the park!

Mr. Cohen drove up to the Thrill Kingdom gate. Frank and Joe helped lift Phil's coaster out of the car. Phil stretched his neck to peer over the Popsicle-stick tracks.

"Are you sure you don't need help carrying your coaster, Phil?" Mr. Cohen asked.

"No thanks, Dad," Phil said. "I've got Frank and Joe to help."

Joe flexed an arm muscle. "And we're strong like bulls, Mr. Cohen!" he said with a grin.

Mr. Cohen wished Phil luck before driving away. The boys flashed their badges at the booth, then walked through the gate. Thrill Kingdom was packed with people enjoying the rides, games, and food.

Joe tried not to look at the Tarantula as they made their way to the contest hall. But as he aimed his eyes straight ahead, he saw something just as creepy: three beefy-looking pirates waving swords and charging straight toward them!

"Avast!" the biggest pirate shouted. "Ye bilge-sucking scalawags!"

2

Winners—and Losers!

Frank, Joe, and Phil stopped in their tracks as the pirates charged over.

"My allowance is in my back pocket!" Phil blurted out to the pirates towering over them. "But don't take my Zooming Zombie Coaster!"

The three pirates lifted their eye patches to study Phil's ride model.

"Awesome coaster, dude," the red-haired pirate with freckles said. "I'll bet it's for that lame contest."

"What's so lame about it?" Frank demanded.

"Duh!" the pirate with the skull and crossbones tattoo said. "The winning ride replaces Buccaneer Cove."

Frank studied the swords. They were plastic, not steel. And the pirates' tattoos looked stuck on. As Frank looked closer he saw that the pirates were no older than nineteen!

"Buccaneer Cove is neat," Joe admitted. "I like

that spinning barrel we have to run through, and the trick mirrors."

Then Joe nodded at Phil's Zooming Zombie Coaster and said, "But you're looking at the ride that's about to take its place. The Zooming Zombie Coaster!"

Phil jabbed Joe with his elbow, but it was too late. The pirates were already glaring at Phil's ride model.

"Um . . . nothing personal, maties!" Phil told the pirates. "But we've got to ship off now!"

"Not so fast!" The biggest pirate shoved his fake but still-sharp sword in front of the boys.

"Sign this first," the red-haired pirate said, holding out a clipboard. "It's a petition to save Buccaneer Cove."

"If we get enough people to sign," the pirate with the tattoo said, "we'll save Buccaneer Cove— and our jobs."

Frank, Joe, and Phil traded glances. The contest was to *replace* Buccaneer Cove, not save it. Signing the petition wouldn't make sense!

Thinking fast, Frank said, "We can't. We're only eight and nine, so we need our parents' permission to sign anything."

"Or maybe," the biggest pirate said, staring down at Phil's Zooming Zombie Coaster, "you just want to *win*!"

Frank and Joe stared up at the pirates. They knew they weren't real pirates. Just real creepy.

"Um—fair winds, me hearties!" Joe said quickly.

With that, Joe, Frank, and Phil scooted around the pirates and into the crowd.

"Whoa!" Frank said, not looking back. "I might miss Buccaneer Cove when it's gone. But I sure won't miss those pirates."

The brothers and Phil didn't have far to go to the contest hall. It was a red-brick building with a yellow roof and lots of windows. Inside, a big room was decorated with silver and gold balloons. Two long tables were set up for the ride models. Another smaller table held awesome-looking cupcakes!

A tall woman wearing khaki pants and a white blouse smiled as she walked over. "Hi, guys," she said. "I'm Nina Milton, the contest director. You can start setting up your ride model on one of the tables."

"Then can we have a cupcake?" Joe asked. He felt Frank nudge him with his elbow and quickly added, "Please?"

"Sure!" Nina smiled. "Help yourselves."

After carefully setting the Zooming Zombie Coaster down, the boys grabbed chocolate-and-peanut-butter cupcakes. Frank and Phil finished theirs in a few bites. Joe was still licking away at his as they checked out the other ride models.

The boys recognized some kids from school.

Dana Philips had built a miniature carousel with dinosaurs instead of horses. Kevin Singh had modeled a silver space shuttle inside a diorama of outer space. Keisha Cromley from Joe's third-grade class had built a miniature fun house.

"A fun house?" Joe whispered to Frank. "Why does she think they would replace Buccaneer Cove with another fun house?"

Suddenly Frank spotted someone from his fourth-grade class. It was Daisy Zamora. Daisy was

setting up her ride model next to Phil's. She wore a bright yellow T-shirt that read IN IT TO WIN IT!

"Everybody here wants to win," Joe said.

"Not as much as Daisy Zamora!" Frank said, lowering his voice so she wouldn't hear. "She's supercompetitive."

"Hey, Frank!" Daisy called, waving them over. "Check out my spinning pizza ride."

She gave the plastic pizza on a stick a whack.

The boys grinned as it began spinning around and around.

"Hey," Phil said, "don't your mom and dad own the Leaning Tower of Pizza parlor on Water Street?"

"Does *this* answer your question?" Daisy said.

She held up her wrist to show a red rubber bracelet. Stamped around it were the words LEAN-ING TOWER OF PIZZA. "We also run a pizza stand right here in the park."

"Neat!" Joe said. "I'll bet you get to ride all the rides for free!"

Daisy rolled her eyes. "I may get free pizza and garlic knots," she said. "But I have to buy ride tickets just like everybody else."

Daisy began spinning the pizza harder and much faster. "That's why I *have* to win this contest," she said. "And I'll do anything to win. *Anything!*"

The Hardys and Phil traded glances. Daisy Zamora meant business.

Suddenly two smaller kids barged past Joe to the table.

"Out of our way, out of our way!" one of them demanded.

Joe almost dropped his chocolate-and-peanut-butter cupcake. They looked exactly alike—identical twins!

"What are you doing here, Matty and Scotty?" Daisy asked, annoyed. "You're supposed to be at the pizza stand with Mom and Dad."

"We want to help you with the contest!" Matty said. His small blue backpack bounced as he jumped up and down. "Can we? Can we? Huuuuh?"

"Matty can spin the pizza!" Scotty added. "And I'll make sure nobody eats it!"

"No one is going to eat a plastic pizza!" Daisy snapped. "And I told you—you're too young for this contest. You're both six, and you have to be eight!"

Scotty tapped his chin as he thought. His eyes lit up as he said, "If you add our ages together, we're ten!"

"Twelve!" Matty whispered to his twin.

"Nice try," Daisy said with a smirk. "Go find another contest!"

Pouting, the twins backed away from the table. But when they looked at Phil's ride model, their eyes lit up again.

"What's that?" Scotty gasped.

"It's my Zooming Zombie Coaster," Phil answered. "It's made out of hundreds of Freezy Fruity Popsicle sticks."

The twins traded smiles. As they whirled around to leave, Matty's backpack hit Joe in the stomach. Before Joe could complain, the twins were out the door.

"Little brothers," Daisy sighed. "I can't think of bigger pests."

"I can!" Frank whispered. "Look who just walked in."

"Who?" Joe asked. He followed Frank's gaze and groaned. Walking into the contest hall like he owned the place was Bayport's biggest bully, Adam Ackerman!

Following Adam were his buds Tony Riccio and Seth Darnell. Adam was shouting orders to them as they lugged a silver coaster model to one of the tables.

Joe took a slow lick of the frosting on his cupcake as he eyed Adam's coaster. Where had he seen that thing before?

"Hey, Cohen," Adam shouted when he saw Phil. "My coaster wipes the floor with yours any day!"

Suddenly Joe remembered where he'd seen the coaster. "Hey, Adam," he called, "isn't that from the build-it-yourself kit? You know, the one at Toys 4 Us?"

In a flash Adam was in Joe's face. He grabbed Joe by the front of his T-shirt and lifted him right off his feet.

"Keep your mouth shut, Hardy!" Adam growled. "Or you'll be sorry!"

Coaster Shocker

L et him go, Adam!" Frank shouted.

"You heard him," Joe squeaked, clutching his cupcake.

Tony, Seth, and more kids ran over. So did Nina Milton. "What on earth is going on here?" she demanded.

Adam let go of Joe. He plopped onto the floor.

"We were just fighting over the last cupcake," Adam mumbled. He pointed to Joe's cupcake, now splattered on the floor. "No big deal."

"Doubtful," Nina said. She frowned as she pointed at the snack table. "There are still plenty of cupcakes left."

"Joe and I were wondering if Adam's coaster came from a kit," Frank said. He flashed Adam a glare. "No big deal."

"Adam?" Nina asked. "Is your model from a kit?"

"No way!" Adam declared. He pointed a finger at Frank and Joe. "They're just playing detective again!"

Joe was about to argue—until Tony blurted out, "But it is from a kit, Adam. It took me all weekend to build it, remember?"

Adam clapped his hand over Tony's mouth, but it was too late.

"So the cat's out of the bag!" Frank said.

"You mean the coaster's out of the box!" Joe added.

"What difference does it make where it came

from?" Adam snapped, his face red. "It's an awesome coaster!"

Nina shook her head. "Adam, I'm afraid you're disqualified from the contest," she said.

"What?" Adam cried.

"Return your badges, please," Nina said, holding out her hand. "Then leave the contest hall with your coaster."

Adam, Tony, and Seth grumbled as they handed their badges to Nina. After Nina walked away, Adam turned to Frank. "I told you not to open your big mouth!" he growled.

"You told Joe, not me," Frank said, staring Adam down. "So why don't you take your bogus coaster—and roll!"

"Come on, Adam," Seth said. "You don't need this dumb contest."

Adam shot the Hardys one last glare before following his friends.

"I know that look," Frank whispered. "It's the Adam Ackerman look of revenge."

"Great," Joe muttered. Now he had two things to worry about: the Tarantula ride—and Adam Ackerman!

It was twelve thirty when all the ride models were set up. Nina raised her hands for attention, then made an announcement: "The contest is at five o'clock. Until then you can ride any of the rides in the park for free."

"Cool!" Joe cheered with the others.

The contestants had to be back at two o'clock to have their pictures taken for the *Bayport News*, and again at four thirty to prepare for the big contest.

"Do we leave our ride models here?" Phil asked in a worried voice.

"We don't want them stolen!" Kevin said.

"Both doors will be locked," Nina promised.

"Now go have fun and don't worry about a thing."

Frank, Joe, and Phil left the contest hall with the other contestants. Once outside, Joe glanced around. "Where do you think Adam went?" he whispered.

"Probably riding some monster ride," Frank scoffed.

"Takes a monster to ride one," Joe said. He smiled and waved his hand in the direction of the rides. "Come on, you guys. Let's rock the Bodacious Bobsled!"

On the way the boys ran into their friends Chet and Iola Morton.

"Where are you guys headed?" Frank asked.

"The Tarantula!" Chet said, his eyes flashing.

"Our goal is to ride it a dozen times this summer!" Chet's sister, Iola, said excitedly. "Want to come?"

"No!" Joe blurted out. "I mean . . . no thanks."

Chet and Iola hurried off for the Tarantula. Frank turned to Joe and said, "You'd better get used to the idea. Phil's coaster is going to win, and you remember our deal?"

"How can I forget?" Joe asked, irritated.

The brothers and Phil rode a half dozen rides, starting with the Bodacious Bobsled. Somewhere between the Winding Wildebeest and the Trip to Mars, Joe got hungry for his favorite thrill-park snack: honey-roasted nuts!

"Be right back!" Joe told Frank and Phil. He ran to find a nut vendor. There were carts selling Italian ices, hot dogs, and candy, but not one selling nuts.

Joe was about to settle for a bag of jumbo jaw-breakers when he was almost knocked down by three guys running like the wind.

"Out of the way, sea-snake!" a voice growled.

They were the pirates from Buccaneer Cove. The biggest pirate was carrying something under his arm. It looked like an old-fashioned pirate treasure chest!

"Pirates," Joe sighed. He bought a small bag of jawbreakers and shoved it inside his pocket. Then he ran to join Frank and Phil.

"It's about time!" Phil complained.

"Hey, remember those pirates we saw?" Joe started to say. "I saw them running—"

"Who cares about the pirates?" Frank said. "We've got exactly five minutes to get back to the contest hall!"

"We can do it in four," Joe declared. "Let's go!"

Frank, Joe, and Phil raced through the crowds. They made it to the contest hall in less than five minutes. But when they walked inside, something was definitely not right.

Nina, the judges, and the other kids were crowded around Phil's Zooming Zombie Coaster, and this time they were not smiling.

"Hey, guys," Joe said. "What's up?"

Everyone turned to stare at Phil and backed away from the table. The boys gasped. A huge chunk of the Zooming Zombie Coaster was missing!

4

Sticks and Groans

My coaster!" Phil wailed. "My Zooming Zombie Coaster is ruined!"

Frank and Joe were too stunned to speak.

"How did that happen?" Frank finally asked.

The other contestants shook their heads. Joe turned to Nina. "Excuse me, but did you lock the doors?" he asked. "Like you said you would?"

"I most certainly did," Nina insisted. "When

the judges and I got back from lunch, we found Phil's coaster like this."

Frank's eyes darted around the contest hall. He spotted an open window. "Somebody could have climbed through that window to get to Phil's coaster," he said.

"Or maybe it was just an accident," Nina said. "Somebody could have bumped into the coaster on the way out."

"Not me," Daisy said.

"Me neither," Keisha piped up.

Joe walked around the wrecked coaster. He checked out the floor all around and underneath the table.

"What are you looking for?" Daisy asked.

"Popsicle sticks," Joe replied. "I don't see any loose Popsicle sticks anywhere."

"So?" Nina asked.

"So if the coaster fell apart," Frank jumped in

to explain, "the missing Popsicle sticks would be around here somewhere."

"Exactly!" Joe nodded.

"What are you," Nina chuckled, "some kind of detectives?"

"Yes," the other contestants confirmed.

"Then where are the missing Popsicle sticks?" Phil said. "They couldn't have just disappeared."

"Whoever did this probably got rid of the Popsicle sticks," Joe said. "To get rid of the evidence."

"You mean somebody did this on *purpose*?" Phil asked.

"Looks that way, Phil," Frank said. "The big question is: Who did it?"

Phil narrowed his eyes and looked straight at Joe. "I'll tell you who did it," he said angrily.

"Me?" Joe cried, surprised.

With a nod, Phil said, "You told Frank and me you were going to look for nuts," Phil said. "You never got any because you had other plans!"

Joe lifted the plastic bag from his pocket. "I got jawbreakers instead, see?" he said. "And what plans are you talking about?"

"Yeah, Phil," Frank said. "Don't tell me you think Joe ruined your Zooming Zombie Coaster."

"I *know* he did it!" Phil insisted. "Joe didn't want me to win because he's too chicken to ride the Tarantula!"

The other kids snickered. One boy clucked like a chicken. Joe was so embarrassed, he wanted to disappear!

"Come on, Phil, you're one of our best buds," Frank said with a smile. "How can you accuse Joe?"

"Yeah!" Joe said. "I didn't eat all those Freezy Fruity pops for nothing."

"That was before the dare!" Phil snapped.

Then—FLASH! A quick and bright light filled the room. Everyone turned to see a guy holding a camera.

"Who are you?" Nina asked the man.

"Reporter from the *Bayport News*," he replied. "I'm here to take pictures and report on the contest."

He aimed his camera at Phil's ruined Zooming Zombie Coaster and said, "Mind if I get a shot of the vandalism?"

Nina gasped at the word "vandalism."

"Absolutely not!" Nina said. "There will be no bad press on this contest."

She then turned to the kids. "And there will be no contest until the person responsible for the damage steps forward," she said.

Disappointed groans filled the room. Frank and Joe stared at each other. Would the guilty person ever step forward?

"You've got until four thirty," Nina went on. "And I hope honesty will prevail."

"No contest?" Daisy wailed as Nina walked away. "But I've got to win!"

"No contest, no Tarantula," Phil said to Joe. "Looks like you got your wish."

Joe watched as Phil huffed over to his vandalized coaster. "How could Phil accuse me?" he asked Frank.

"Phil is upset about his coaster," Frank said.

"He probably doesn't know what he's saying."

Joe gestured toward other kids glaring at him.

"But now everybody is blaming me for the contest getting canceled," Joe whispered. "Thanks to Phil, they think I did it."

"Not if we find the real person who did it," Frank whispered back. "We're detectives, right?"

"Right," Joe said.

"We've found missing a softball mitt, stolen money, and a lost pet," Frank said. "For sure we can find the real creep who messed with Phil's coaster. Right?"

"Right!" Joe said, feeling better.

"Not only will we save the contest," Frank said, "we'll save our friendship with Phil."

"And *me* from being thrill-park enemy number one!" Joe said. He then forced a smile. "So what are we waiting for, Frank? Let's crack this crazy case."

5

When . . . What . . . Who?

"T oo bad Nina wouldn't let us stay inside the contest hall," Joe said as he and Frank walked through Thrill Kingdom. "We always start by looking for clues."

Frank shook his head. "We always start by filling in the six *W*s," he said. "Who, What, Where, When, Why, and How."

"Which we always write on the whiteboard in our tree house," Joe said. "Where are we going to write them around here?"

"There!" Frank spoke so suddenly that Joe jumped. He pointed to a chalkboard by the small lake behind Buccaneer Cove. The lake was where the fun house's pirate ship sailed. The chalkboard in front of the dock read NEXT CRUISE 3:30.

"There's a piece of chalk hanging from the board," Frank pointed out as he and Joe raced over.

Joe glanced around for pirates. The coast was clear. He grabbed the blue chalk and began writing the six *W*s on the chalkboard.

"The first *W* is What," Joe said as he scribbled. "*What* happened?"

"That's easy," Frank said. "Phil's Zooming Zombie Coaster was vandalized."

Joe wrinkled his nose. "How do you spell vandal—"

"Just write 'messed up,'" Frank interrupted.

Joe wrote quickly. The next *W* was Where. The brothers agreed that was a no-brainer. The

scene of the crime was the contest hall.

"When did it happen?" Joe asked next.

Figuring out the time line was always tricky. "We all left the contest hall at twelve thirty," Frank said.

"And were back a little before two o'clock," Joe added. "So it probably happened sometime between twelve thirty and two o'clock."

The chalk made a squeaking noise as Joe scribbled down the time line.

"Next *W* is Why," Frank said. "Why would anyone want to ruin Phil's coaster?"

"Because it was the best." Joe shrugged. "Someone might have been jealous."

"Or maybe it was an act of revenge," Frank said.

"Which leads us straight to Adam Ackerman," Joe said. "Adam was mad that we told the truth about his coaster."

"Adam also knows Phil is our friend," Frank agreed. "He could have wrecked his coaster to get even with us."

Joe wrote Adam's name on the board.

"We usually have more than one suspect," Frank said. "Who else could have done it?"

Joe thought about the other contestants. Everybody wanted to win. But there was one person who wanted to win more than anything.

"Daisy Zamora!" Joe exclaimed. "Didn't she tell us she'd do anything to win?"

Frank shook his head. "Daisy never cheats in contests," he said. "She always wins fair and square."

"FAIR AND SQUARE! FAIR AND SQUARE! ARRRRRK!"

The high-pitched squawking voice made the brothers spin around. They smiled when they saw—

"Crackers!" Joe said. "It's Crackers the parrot!"

Frank and Joe smiled at the green, red, and yellow parrot. The bird was perched in front of the entrance to Buccaneer Cove like he was every summer.

"I might not miss the pirates when they tear down this place," Frank said, "but I'll sure miss Crackers."

"Pirates!" Joe gasped.

"What about them?" Frank asked.

"I just remembered," Joe said. "The pirates were running with some kind of treasure chest. Maybe the Popsicle sticks were inside!"

"Were they running near the contest hall?" Frank asked.

"They were running *away* from the contest hall," Joe remembered.

"Why didn't you tell me?" Frank asked.

"I tried, but you wouldn't listen!" Joe retorted.

Frank lowered his voice in case there were pirates around. "The pirates had a motive," he said. "They didn't want any ride to replace Buccaneer Cove."

"BUCCANEER COVE! BUCCANEER COVE! ENTER AT YOUR OWN RISK! SQUAAAAAWK!" Crackers screeched.

"Shh!" Joe hissed.

"The pirates were mad that we wouldn't sign

their petition too," Frank went on. "That makes two motives."

"But how would they fit through the window?" Joe asked. "The windows were only half-open, and those pirates are pretty big."

"They wouldn't have had to climb through," Frank said. "They work at Thrill Kingdom, so they could have gotten the keys."

Joe added the pirates to their list of Who. With the clues they already had, it was time to try to crack the case.

"We've got to go inside Buccaneer Cove, find the pirates' treasure chest, and see what's inside," Frank said.

"What if the pirates find us?" Joe whispered. "Their swords may be fake—but their muscles aren't."

"Are you chickening out of this, too?" Frank asked.

"I'm not chickening out!" Joe insisted. "And I'm not afraid of a bunch of stupid pirates—"

"Avast, landlubbers!" a voice shouted.

Joe jumped. A pirate wearing a white blouse, long skirt, and boots marched over. She wore a sparkly purple eye patch and a tiara made from fake bones. Her black T-shirt read PIRATE QUEEN.

She frowned as she pointed to the scribbled-on chalkboard. "What are you doing?" she demanded.

Joe dropped the chalk. He rubbed the six *W*s off with the back of his fist and said, "Um . . . we were just leaving. And a yo-ho-ho to you, too, Your Majesty!"

The brothers raced away from the dock. Crackers screeched as they stopped outside the fun house entrance.

"Now remember, Joe, we're not going inside to have fun," Frank whispered. "We want to find that treasure chest and see what's inside."

"Got it," Joe said.

"GOT IT! GOT IT! RAAAAAAAK!"

"Shh!" Joe hissed.

Frank opened the heavy wooden door. As they entered the fun house, so did Crackers. He landed on the shoulder of a beefy pirate standing right inside the door.

"Aaaargh!" the pirate growled as he held out his hand. "Tickets."

Frank and Joe held up their contest badges.

"Enter," the pirate cackled. "If you dare!"

Frank forced a smile and said, "Thanks."

The brothers walked through the entrance hall. The walls were decorated with nets, fake shark heads, and portraits of grinning, gold-toothed pirates.

Frank and Joe stared up at the portraits.

"Don't you feel like they're watching us?" Joe asked.

"That's because we *are* watching you!" a voice snarled.

Frank and Joe whirled around. The three pirates with the swords were standing right behind them.

"If it isn't the kids from the contest!" The red-haired pirate laughed.

"Change your mind about the petition?" the biggest pirate asked.

"Not a chance," Frank said firmly.

"We're here to . . . to . . . ," Joe started to say—until Crackers swooped over and squawked:

"SEE WHAT'S IN THE TREASURE CHEST! SEE WHAT'S IN THE TREASURE CHEST! ARRRRRRRK!"

"Big-mouthed parrot!" Joe muttered.

The biggest pirate glared with his one eye at the brothers. "So ye want to find our treasaaaargh, huh?" he snarled.

"We never surrendaaaargh our treasaaaargh

without a hearty fight!" the pirate with the tattoo
growled.

With that, the three pirates drew their fake—
but scary—swords.

Joe gulped. He felt Frank grab his arm and
heard him shout, "Come on, Joe! Run!"

6

Fun House Fright

atch it!" a boy shouted as Frank and Joe pushed through a crowd of kids.

Frank and Joe didn't have to look back to know the pirates were chasing them.

"Keep looking for the treasure chest, Joe," Frank called as they thundered up a wooden gangplank.

"We don't have a clue where it is!" Joe called back.

The creaky gangplank led straight to the Spinning Barrel. The barrel was big enough for about six kids to run through—if they *could* run.

Frank glanced over his shoulder. The three pirates were running up the gangplank. The only escape was through the barrel and out the other side!

The barrel was empty when Frank and Joe jumped inside. They tried to run, but the spinning made them slip, stumble, and slide!

"Whooooaaaa!" Frank cried.

"Aaaaaah!" Joe shouted.

Slowly, the brothers finally inched their way to the other side.

"It's spinning faster!" Joe yelled.

Frank looked back. The three pirates were standing outside the barrel, laughing it up.

"They cranked up the speed!" Frank groaned.

The pirates dove inside the barrel. Joe felt sick as the pirates slowly made their way forward. What would they do now? The spinning barrel suddenly threw Joe against his side. He felt the bag of jawbreakers in his pocket.

"Jawbreakers!" Joe cried. "That's it!"

"What are you doing?" Frank called as Joe spilled the hard, round candies out of the bag.

"Watch!" Joe called back.

It wasn't long before the pirates began slipping and sliding over the rolling jawbreakers!

THIS WAY!

"Arrrrrghh!" the pirates yelled.

While the three buccaneers fell flat on their backs, the brothers jumped out of the barrel.

Leaving the pirates to spin, the brothers raced through the next room of the fun house. It was the Crazy Crystal Room, filled with trick mirrors.

"No treasure chest in here!" Frank called to Joe.

Joe stopped running to gaze at one of the mirrors. "Hey, Frank, check it out!" he laughed. "I look like a piece of stretched-out bubble gum!"

Joe stopped laughing when he saw something else in the mirror. The pirates standing right behind him!

"So, what's this about a treasure chest?" the biggest pirate said as they surrounded Joe.

"Leave him alone!" Frank shouted. He was about to call for help when—

"Daddy!" a voice shouted.

Frank turned to see a little girl. She was tugging

her father's sleeve with one hand and pointing at Joe with the other.

"Daddy, those pirates captured that boy!" the girl said in a frightened voice. "Make them stop!"

"Are you okay, young man?" the father asked Joe.

All three pirates turned away from Joe.

"We meant no harm, sir!" the biggest pirate said, putting on a smile. "It's all part of the act here, you see."

"Sure!" the pirate with the tattoo said. "We're really friendly pirates."

The pirates tried to cheer the little girl up by singing a goofy sea shanty. Frank and Joe used the moment to escape.

"Friendly pirates, yeah, right," Frank muttered as they ran into the next room—the one with the tilted deck!

"Whooaaa!" Joe cried as they tried to run across a slanted floor. "And they call this a fun house?"

Frank glanced around the room for the treasure chest. All he saw were more kids and two doors, also slanted.

"Maybe the chest is behind one of those doors," Frank said. "You open the red, and I'll open the yellow!"

Joe yanked the red door open. He screamed as a grinning skeleton tumbled out.

"It's fake, Joe!" Frank said. He pulled open the yellow door. He screamed too as a slimy squidlike creature bobbed out.

"We'd better go before those pirates get here!" Joe said. "Come on."

"Wait," Frank said. He nodded at another door in the corner of the room. "We didn't look behind that one."

Joe stared at the door and a sign that read CREW ONLY! LANDLUBBERS BEWARE!

"It's for the pirates," Joe said with a frown.

"Exactly!" Frank said. "They could have stashed the treasure chest behind there."

Luckily, the door wasn't locked. It led to a long hallway. The boys ran down the hall, which led to a big room filled with racks of costumes and shelves of props.

Joe smiled as he checked out the fake hook hands, pirate hats, and boxes of eye patches. He popped a hat on his head, squeezed one eye shut, and growled, "Arrrrgggh!"

"Will you quit playing, Joe?" Frank snapped. "Look for the treasure chest."

Joe scrambled to help his brother look for the treasure chest. He smiled when he came upon a black cloth draped over an object on the floor.

"What every pirate needs," Joe said, grabbing hold of the cloth. "A swashbuckling cape!"

"Joe!" Frank said. "I told you—quit playing!"

But when Joe pulled the cloth, both brothers

gasped. Underneath was a treasure chest!

"That's the one I saw the pirates carrying," Joe said excitedly. "Let's see if the Popsicle sticks are inside."

The brothers got down on their knees. They tried to pry the lid open, but . . .

"It's locked!" Joe said.

"Maybe it's stuck," Frank said. He gritted his teeth as he gripped the edge of the lid.

Then—*plop*!

Frank and Joe yelled as a thick and heavy net dropped down over them.

"We're trapped, Frank!" Joe said as they struggled with the tangled net.

"That's the idea," a gruff voice said.

Frank and Joe froze.

They peered through the net at the three pirates standing at the door. The biggest pirate had Crackers on his shoulder. The red-haired

pirate clutched a rope hanging from the ceiling—
the rope that probably dropped the net.

"I see ye found our treasaaaaaargh!" the biggest pirate said.

"Yeah," Joe muttered. "And I guess you
found *us*."

7

Thrill-Park Chase

Raaak!" Crackers squawked as the pirates approached the captured Hardys.

"What's inside the treasure chest?" Frank demanded through the net. "Is it Phil's Popsicle sticks?"

The tattooed pirate wrinkled his nose as if he didn't get it. "Did you say 'Popsicle sticks'?" he said.

Joe stopped struggling with the net as he took

a whiff. "Frank?" he whispered. "I think I smell chocolate."

"So?" Frank said.

"Peanut butter, too," Joe said with another sniff. "And I think it's coming from inside the treasure chest."

Both brothers stared down at the pirates' secret treasure chest. They moved around to the back of the chest. There they found four big fudgy-looking fingerprints on the pale wood.

"Fruity Freezy pops don't come in chocolate and peanut butter," Joe pointed out.

"Chocolate . . . peanut butter," Frank repeated. His eyes lit up. "The cupcakes!"

"Oh, rats," the biggest pirate muttered.

"Aha—so that's it!" Joe said through the net. "You didn't steal Popsicle sticks—you stole our cupcakes!"

"HIDE THE CUPCAKES! HIDE THE CUPCAKES!" Crackers screeched. "AAARK!"

Frank frowned at the pirates through the net. "Game over, dudes," he said.

"Now get us out of here!" Joe said, shaking the net.

The pirates no longer sounded like pirates as they peeled the heavy net off the Hardys.

"The net's something we rigged up for laughs," the tattooed pirate said. "It was meant for the other pirates, not you guys."

The red-haired pirate rapped on the lid of the treasure chest. It sprung open to reveal about a dozen cupcakes.

"We saw the bakery load them into the contest hall this morning," the biggest pirate said. "They looked awesome, so we took a few."

"You mean you stole them!" Frank said.

"Not really," the red-haired pirate said. "When we peeked inside the contest hall, everybody was gone."

"Couldn't let all those cupcakes go to waste," the biggest pirate said. "So we got the key and helped ourselves."

"If you weren't doing anything wrong," Joe asked, "why'd you hide them in that treasure chest?"

"Hey, we're pirates!" the biggest pirate said. "And you must be those kid detectives we heard about in town . . . the Smarty brothers?"

"Hardy," Frank corrected.

"Well, Hardys," the tattooed pirate said with a grin, "want some cupcakes for your trouble?"

Frank and Joe glanced down at the cupcakes. After being inside a hot, stuffy treasure chest, they were a mushy mess!

"Um, no thanks," Frank said.

"We'd better get going," Joe said.

The red-haired pirate pointed to a door. "That door leads outside. So you won't have to run through that barrel again."

Frank and Joe were grateful for the shortcut. They were also grateful that the mean pirates had turned out to be nice guys. And were no longer suspects!

"I guess that leaves us with Adam Ackerman,"

Frank said as he and Joe walked away from the fun house.

"Adam—and Daisy," Joe said.

"Daisy?" Frank asked.

"The Zamoras have a pizza stand right here in Thrill Kingdom," Joe said. "She could have gotten a key too!"

"I told you, Daisy Zamora is not a suspect, Joe," Frank insisted. "Now let's look for Adam."

The brothers looked around the park for Adam and his friends. Joe stopped when he spotted a cart selling honey-roasted nuts. What he spotted next made his eyes open wide.

"Frank, look who's standing in line to buy nuts!" Joe whispered. "Seth and Tony!"

Frank looked at those lined up at the nut cart. Toward the back of the line, Seth and Tony were counting change in their hands.

"Where do you think Adam is?" Joe whispered.

"I don't know," Frank said, glaring at the boys. "But I'm pretty sure who does!"

Frank and Joe headed over to Adam's friends.

"If you want nuts, get in line!" Tony said.

"We just want one nut," Joe said. "Adam Ackerman!"

"Where is he?" Frank demanded.

"He left with his coaster hours ago," Seth said.

"Why would Adam leave?" Frank said. "You guys are still here."

"They *made* Adam leave!" Tony said. "For splashing a blue slushie all over Chet Morton."

Joe wrinkled his nose. "Adam did that?" he said.

"They should have made him leave for wrecking Phil's ride model," Frank said angrily.

"And you guys probably helped," Joe added.

"What are you talking about?" Tony asked. He turned to Seth. "This line is too long—let's go."

Tony and Seth began walking away. Frank and Joe followed.

"We know Adam's still here!" Frank called after them. "And we know *you* know!" Joe shouted.

Adam's friends picked up speed as they pushed their way through the crowd.

"If they go on a ride, so do we," Frank told Joe as they hurried after the two.

"You bet, Frank!" Joe agreed. "You bet."

Then Tony and Seth headed straight toward . . . the Tarantula!

8

Big Blue Clue

Will you come on?" Frank said, tugging Joe's arm. "If we hurry, we can get in the same cage as Seth and Tony!"

Joe's feet stayed planted on the ground. He wasn't going anywhere—especially not on the Tarantula!

"I can't, Frank," Joe said.

"But you said you'd go on the Tarantula!" Frank said.

Joe yanked his arm back. "*If* Phil wins the

contest," he said. "The contest hasn't even started yet. It might not even happen!"

Frank groaned as Seth and Tony taunted them, waving from their cage. "We could have been right in their faces, Joe!" he said. "We could have found out where Adam really is."

"They've got to get off sooner or later," Joe said. "Unless . . . Seth and Tony were telling the truth."

"The truth?" Frank asked.

"Maybe Adam *did* get kicked out of the park for pouring a slushie on Chet," Joe said.

Time was running out as the brothers set out to find Chet. But where would they find Chet and Iola Morton in a park filled with people?

"Let's think," Frank said as they walked past the Tilt-a-Whirl and the Dizzy Lizzy rides. "Chet and Iola have probably ridden most of the rides by now."

"They might be at the carnival games!" Joe said, snapping his fingers.

The brothers found the row of carnival games. Joe checked out the kids playing whack-a-mole, beanbag toss, wheel of fortune, and the hoop toss. No Chet or Iola. Until Frank said, "There he is!"

Standing at the balloon squirt game were Chet and Iola. The brother and sister stood perfectly still as they blasted water into the open mouths of rubber clown heads. The balloon that filled up with water and popped first would win.

"Yo, Chet!" Joe called as they ran over.

"Huh?" Chet whirled around, the blaster still in his hands.

"Chet, watch it!" Joe shouted as water blasted straight at him. He ducked, but not fast enough. His hair was sopping wet, water dripping down his face!

"Sorry about that," Chet said after Iola's balloon popped and the water stopped. "But you got me right in the middle of a game."

"And I won, I won!" Iola cheered. She held up her new giant stuffed panda prize. "Thanks, Joe!"

"Don't mention it." Joe sighed as he wiped his wet face with the bottom of his T-shirt.

Frank stared at Chet's T-shirt and the big stain on the front. The big *blue* stain!

"How did that happen?" Frank asked.

"I was slushied," Chet said with a frown. "Adam Ackerman poured a giant slushie all over me!"

"Just now?" Joe asked excitedly.

Chet shook his head. "Hours ago," he said. "Right after we saw you guys."

"We were about to go on the Tarantula when Adam pushed ahead of us in line," Iola explained. "We tried to make him move back. Instead, the creep poured his whole slushie on Chet," she added angrily.

"Not the whole thing, Iola!" Chet said. "I jumped back and only got about half."

"Whatever." Iola sighed.

"Then what happened?" Joe asked.

"A guard ran over," Iola said. "He told Adam he had to leave Thrill Kingdom."

"Adam Ackerman was led straight to the gate and out of the park," Chet declared.

"Bye-bye, bully!" Iola added with a grin.

Joe gave Frank a sideways glance. Seth and Tony *were* telling the truth.

"Sorry I got you drenched, Joe," Chet said.

"He'll live," Iola told Chet. She gave her giant stuffed panda a squeeze. "Now let's play whack-a-mole while I feel lucky."

Chet and Iola walked back to the carnival games. Frank and Joe did the math.

"Adam was out of the park at the time of the crime," Joe said. "So he couldn't have ruined Phil's coaster."

"Seth and Tony weren't kicked out of the park,"

Frank pointed out. "Maybe they were the ones who did it."

"Yeah, but where did they put all those Popsicle sticks?" Joe said. "We didn't see them holding anything."

"They could have dumped the Popsicle sticks on their way out of the contest hall," Frank said. "Maybe there's a trash can right outside the open window."

Joe glanced at a clock. "Ten minutes after three," he said. "If we're going to solve this case by four thirty, we'd better move it!"

The brothers charged back to the contest hall and hurried around to the back. The window that was open before was now shut and locked. There were no trash cans anywhere near the window.

"What about the other trash cans in the park?" Joe said. "We can dig through those."

"Do you know how many trash cans are in

Thrill Kingdom?" Frank frowned. "Thanks—but no thanks!"

Joe was about to turn away from the window when he spotted something right underneath it. There was a plastic crate turned upside down.

"Whoever climbed through the window needed a boost," Joe pointed out.

"Seth and Tony wouldn't need one," Frank said. "They're tall enough to reach the window."

Joe stared down at the crate. His eyes fell on something bright red. It was curled on the grass next to the crate. "Hey, is that a salamander?" He smiled.

He bent down for a better look. It wasn't a salamander but a red rubber bracelet.

Joe picked up the bracelet. "Where did we see this before?" he asked, handing it to Frank.

Frank read the words stamped on the bracelet out loud: "Leaning Tower of Pizza."

Leaning Tower of Pizza?

Joe's brows flew up. That was Daisy Zamora's family's pizza parlor!

"It's Daisy's bracelet, Frank!" Joe exclaimed. "I told you she did it!"

9

Pizzas, Popsicles—Proof!

Frank stared at the bracelet. He hadn't thought Daisy'd had anything to do with Phil's vandalized coaster—until now!

"What do you think, Frank?" Joe urged.

Frank stuffed the bracelet into his pocket. "I think we'd better find Daisy," he said.

The brothers found Daisy at her parents' pizza stand. Daisy was helping her parents behind the counter, taking orders and handing out slices.

"Have your orders ready!" Daisy shouted to

the people in line. "Okay, who's got the pepperoni with extra cheese?"

Joe's mouth watered when he saw the pizza. "How about some slices while we question Daisy, Frank?" he asked.

"We don't have enough time," Frank insisted. "We have exactly an hour to solve this case!"

Some kids standing in line grumbled as the Hardys made their way to the front.

"I don't care if you're in my class, Frank Hardy," Daisy scolded. "No cutting in line."

"We don't want pizza," Frank said. "We want to ask you some questions."

"About what?" Daisy asked.

"About what happened at the contest," Joe added.

Daisy's curls bounced as she shook her head. "Can't," she said. "I'm working here."

Daisy's dad was pounding a lump of dough.

"Vince and I got it covered, Daisy," he called back.

"Go have fun with your friends."

Vince, a teenager behind the counter, gave Daisy a thumbs-up.

Daisy whipped off her apron, then slipped out of the stand to join the Hardys. They stepped away from the pizza stand as they spoke.

"What's up?" Daisy asked. "Is the contest back on? Did the person who messed up Phil's ride model come clean?"

"I don't know," Joe said. "Did you?"

Daisy stopped walking. So did Frank and Joe.

"Me?" Daisy exclaimed. "I know you guys are detectives, but are you saying I did it?"

"Not yet," Joe said. "That's why we want to ask you some questions."

"Like where were you today between twelve thirty and two o'clock?" Frank asked.

"Right *here*," Daisy insisted. She turned toward the pizza stand and shouted, "Daaaaaaaad! Where was I between twelve thirty and two o'clock?"

Mr. Zamora busily handed out slices as he

shouted back, "You were helping us here! . . . Now who gets mushroom?"

Daisy turned to Frank and Joe and smiled. "See?" she said. "My little brothers wanted my mom to drive them home, so my dad needed help."

"So you were here all that time?" Frank asked.

Daisy sighed. "You heard my dad," she said. "I know you guys are good detectives—but this time you've got it all wrong."

Daisy walked back to the pizza stand.

"Why didn't you show her the bracelet?" Joe asked. "The red bracelet she dropped at the scene of the crime?"

Frank nodded toward Daisy, who was handing a slice of pizza to a kid. Dangling from her wrist was a red rubber bracelet!

"Daisy is still wearing hers," Frank pointed out. "The one we found doesn't belong to her."

"Whose is it, then?" Joe asked.

The brothers walked away from the pizza stand. They didn't get far before Joe made gagging sounds.

"What?" Frank asked.

Joe pointed to the Freezy Fruity Popsicle stand. "I can't stand to look at another one of those pops!" he said.

Frank walked up to a sign next to the stand. "Hey, Joe, check it out," he called over his shoulder. "Freezy Fruity is having a contest."

"What kind of contest?" Joe asked, walking over.

Frank read the rules and said, "The kid who sends in the most Freezy Fruity Popsicle sticks wins a year's supply of Freezy Fruity pops."

"That could have been me!" Joe groaned. "Come on, Frank. We have to figure out who our next suspect is."

"Wait!" Frank said as he read more of the rules.

"It says that contestants have to be at least five years old."

"So?" Joe asked.

"So, Daisy's brothers, Matty and Scotty, are six," Frank said. "Didn't Daisy tell them to find another contest?"

"Yeah," Joe said slowly.

"Matty and Scotty must have known about this contest," Frank said. "The stand is right next to their parents' pizza stand!"

"But how would they know that Phil used Freezy Fruity sticks for his ride model?" Joe asked.

"Phil told them, remember?" Frank said.

"One of them had a backpack, too," Joe recalled. "Perfect for stashing the Popsicle sticks!"

"No wonder they needed a crate to climb in and out of the window," Frank said. "They may be small, but they're big trouble."

"Double trouble!" Joe declared.

"We have to find Matty and Scotty," Frank said.

"Daisy said Matty and Scotty went home with their mom," Joe remembered.

"The Zamoras live right above the Leaning Tower of Pizza," Frank said. "Let's leave the park and go there."

The brothers ran straight to the Thrill Kingdom gate. But just as they were about to race through it, they froze.

"Um . . . we can't leave the park on our own," Frank said.

"Oh . . . yeah," Joe said.

The brothers sulked away from the gate. How would they question Matty and Scotty if they couldn't leave the park?

Suddenly—

"Frank! Joe!" a voice called.

It was a very familiar voice. It was their dad's!

"Dad, what are you doing here?" Joe asked.

"I came to watch the contest," Mr. Hardy replied. "And maybe ride a few rides with my boys!"

"Change of plans, Dad!" Frank said as he and Joe ran to him. "Can you please drive us to the Leaning Tower of Pizza?"

"We'll get our hands stamped so we can get back into the park," Joe said.

"But I just got here!" Mr. Hardy said, surprised.

"It's a case we're working on, Dad," Joe said.

Mr. Hardy stared at the boys, then smiled. "A case, huh?" he said. "Why didn't you say so? Come on, let's go."

The brothers traded grins as they all got their hands stamped. Their detective dad knew the importance of solving cases!

Once inside the car, Frank and Joe told their dad all about the case of the Zooming Zombie Coaster.

"Matty and Scotty are good suspects," Mr. Hardy said as he turned the car onto Water Street. "But remember, they're not guilty until you have proof."

"I think we're about to get proof, Dad," Frank said. He leaned over Joe to point out the backseat window. "Because there they are!"

Joe glanced out the window too. Matty and Scotty were standing next to a mailbox on the sidewalk.

Matty held a big padded envelope. Scotty was jumping up and down trying to reach the mailbox handle.

"What are they mailing?" Joe asked.

"There's only one way to find out!" Frank said.

Mr. Hardy steered the car to the curb. Frank and Joe unbuckled their seat belts and jumped out. Scotty was still trying to reach the handle when Frank and Joe ran over.

"Can we help?" Frank asked Scotty.

"Sure!" Scotty said. He smiled up at Frank, expecting him to open the mailbox. Instead, Frank grabbed the envelope right out of Matty's hands.

"Hey!" Matty shouted. "That's ours!"

\10/

The Winner Is . . .

Frank held the envelope high over Matty's head. Written across the envelope in purple crayon were the words: FREEZY FRUITY CONTEST, USA.

Joe narrowed his eyes at the twins. "Freezy Fruity contest, huh?" he said.

Frank squeezed the envelope. It crunched. "Are there Popsicle sticks inside?" he demanded.

Scotty rolled his eyes. "How else are we going to win the contest?" he said.

Just then Frank noticed a red rubber bracelet around Scotty's wrist. He looked at Matty. There was no bracelet on either of his wrists.

"Joe," Frank hissed, "the bracelet is Matty's."

Joe turned to the twins. "Okay, you guys," he said. "Did those Popsicle sticks come from Phil Cohen's Zooming Zombie Coaster?"

Scotty nodded. "He had tons of them!"

"Enough Popsicle sticks to win," Matty said excitedly. "Daisy told us to enter another contest, so we did."

"Yeah!" Scotty said. He started jumping for the envelope again. "So give us back our Popsicle sticks so we *can* win!"

Frank held the envelope even higher. "You're not winners if you're cheaters!" he said.

"You didn't get the Popsicle sticks by eating Freezy Fruity pops," Joe said. "You stole them from Phil's Zooming Zombie Coaster."

"We didn't steal them—we borrowed them," Matty said, still jumping.

"It's nice to share," Scotty said. "At least, that's what we learned in school."

"But it's *not* nice to break someone's ride model," Joe said.

"If the Freezy Fruity people find out what you did," Frank continued, "you guys could be disqualified."

The twins' eyes popped at the big word. Matty stopped jumping up and down.

"Is that the same as 'arrested'?" Matty said.

"No," Joe said, shaking his head. "But—"

"We didn't think Phil would mind," Scotty cut in.

"He had so many Popsicle sticks!" Matty said. "And it's not like we took all of them."

"But you ruined his ride model," Frank said. "And that's wrong."

Matty and Scotty stared at each other. They burst into tears.

"Will you stop crying?" Joe said. He nodded at the envelope. "We got the Popsicle sticks just in time."

"If we work fast enough, maybe we can help rebuild his coaster in time for the contest," Frank added.

The twins stopped crying and smiled.

"Can we help?" Matty sniffed.

"Sure," Frank said. He nodded toward the Zamoras' apartment above the Leaning Tower of Pizza parlor. "You can start by getting a bottle of glue from your mom."

"You got it, dudes!" Scotty said with a smile.

"And here," Frank said as he pulled the red rubber bracelet from his pocket. "I think this is yours."

Matty grinned as he took the bracelet from Frank. "I was looking for that," he said. "Thanks."

Mr. Hardy wasted no time driving Frank and Joe back to Thrill Kingdom. Matty and Scotty followed with their mom in her car with the bottle of glue and a big bag of garlic knots for Phil, Frank, and Joe.

All four boys raced straight to the Thrill Kingdom office. Nina listened to Matty and Scotty as they apologized and explained everything.

"Apology accepted," Nina said with a smile. "Now the contest can go on as planned."

As for Phil, he accepted Matty and Scotty's apology, as well as the garlic knots and some help rebuilding his Zooming Zombie Coaster. Frank, Joe, and Daisy pitched in too. With so much help, Phil's coaster was ready to roll with five minutes to spare!

"Sorry I blamed you for wrecking my coaster, Joe," Phil said. He held out his hand. "Do you want to shake on it?"

"With glue all over our hands?" Joe said with a smile. "Not a good idea . . . but being friends again is."

Joe and Phil traded fist bumps just as Nina announced it was time for the contest.

Frank and Joe watched as the contest judges checked out the ride models, one by one.

When the judges reached Phil's Zooming Zombie Coaster, Joe whispered to Frank, "Fingers crossed."

CLINK! Phil dropped a marble on the top of his coaster. It rattled all the way down the tracks!

"Nice job, young man," one judge said with a smile.

After checking out Daisy's spinning pizza ride, it was time to announce the winner.

One judge whispered to Nina. She smiled at the contestants and said in a booming voice, "And the winner is . . ."

"Phil Cohen, Phil Cohen, Phil Cohen," Joe whispered.

"Keisha Cromley, for her new-and-improved fun house—Extreme Buccaneers!"

Keisha jumped up and down as the guests cheered. Phil smiled at Frank and Joe and shrugged.

"The fun house?" Joe said, surprised.

"New and improved," Frank said. "I guess a thrill park isn't a thrill park without a fun house."

"And pirates!" Joe added. He smiled at the three pirates from Buccaneer's Cove high-fiving nearby. "Three swashbuckling pirates—and one big-mouthed parrot!"

"RAAAAAAAK!" Crackers squawked.

At the end of the superbusy day, Frank and Joe were zonked. But instead of going straight to bed, they went straight to their tree house. They threw a Nerf ball back and forth as they lounged in beanbag chairs.

"Keisha sure is lucky," Joe said. "Free rides for the rest of the summer."

Frank raised a brow at Joe. "You're pretty lucky too," he said. "Now you won't have to ride the Tarantula!"

Joe smiled at Frank, a gleam in his eye. "Oh yeah?" he said slowly. "And how do you know I'm not riding the Tarantula?"

Frank stared at Joe. "You are?" he said. "When?"

"The next time we go to Thrill Kingdom," Joe declared. "Can't let Aunt Gertrude have all the fun!"

Joe dropped the ball on the floor. He jumped out of his beanbag chair and said, "*We've* got something to celebrate too, you know. Something totally, awesomely huge!"

"What?" Frank asked.

"This!" Joe declared. He walked over to the whiteboard hanging on the wall. He picked up a marker and wrote on the board in big blue letters:

SECRET FILES CASE
9
SOLVED!

Did you **LOVE** this book?

Want to get access to great books for **FREE?**

Join

NANCY DREW AND THE CLUE CREW

Test your detective skills with more Clue Crew cases!

FROM ALADDIN • PUBLISHED BY SIMON & SCHUSTER